www.pictureshowpress.net

Author picture credit: Emily Bryant

SECOND EDITION

ISBN-13: 978-1-7324144-2-6
ISBN-10: 1-7324144-2-4

Broken Hat

Barry Lank

Picture Show Press

"I've been from several places,
And I'm going to be from here."

— Jimmie Rodgers

1.

The town of Broken Hat, California started out with two police departments, the older of which was mine. I took over the Sheriff's office in 1953, before this was really a town. I lived for a while in the office itself, which had been an old ranch house—a series of rooms that seemed to have been added one upon the other at different times, each one smelling of wood and long-ago varnish heated by the sun. It seemed like, to the end, I kept finding new empty rooms that I never expected. The front parlor doubled as the post office, and my duties included sorting through the few pieces of mail we'd receive once a week—mostly catalogues, along with the occasional letter in simple Spanish for one of the cowhands.

After a fashion, I was able to buy three acres and a farm of my own near the south hills, on the condition that I figured out my own plumbing and electricity. Since temperatures in the San Gabriel Valley never really dropped to freezing even in dead February, the electricity could really be foregone indefinitely. In winters, I'd just close up the windows—and in summers I'd open them up again, waking to a transparent smell of dry grass.

This had been ranchland for more than a hundred

years, from when this land was still part of Mexico. Wide stretches of dust and hard mud marked where the cattle had grazed, and patches of yellow straw held onto the hills where the cattle had yet to go. Brown cows with white patches on their chests would wander like old drunks into neighboring farms. I caught a heifer poking her head through my kitchen window, licking a now empty plate of pickles.

But the cows were the innocents. Most of my efforts—and probably most of the efforts of sheriffs going back those same hundred-or-so years—focused on the ranch hands. They were day workers, itinerants, ex-cons, grammar school drop-outs and vacationing students who would flip over their cars because they thought it'd be funny to try herding the cows with a 1940 Willys Coupe. Sometimes I found myself having to preserve one of the ranch hands against all the others because he was absolutely useless at work, like this one chattery kid who should have been a lawyer but, for some reason, wasn't. To my relief, he left quickly.

A lot of other people came and went. Some ranch hands had been in one of the last couple wars, and had been floating ever since. This was good work for those guys, and I always hoped they'd hang on. But the more enthusiastic somebody seemed on the first week, the less likely they'd last the month. The men with spark and ambition usually also left, as did anyone who noticed how many new towns were replacing the old ranches nearby. These guys would get smart and move on to a different line of work. That left the ranch hands who were too old to change or too dumb to care—so dumb, they didn't know they were dumb, bragging and razzing each other and blathering about cars and old grudges and baseball. Some would make themselves feel bigger by harassing the ranch hands from Mexico. Not that a lot of our Mexican imports were a whole lot smarter, though. Once I understood a little Spanish, I realized some of these kids came from remote little pueblos and had never seen a tractor before.

At the time, I did not realize I would miss these idiots

later on. I just knew my options for dealing with them were a little narrow. I myself had left behind half my right foot in Pyongtaek, so a lot of these boys could easily outrun me. I thus relied heavily on Guillermo Calderon, the ranch manager. No matter how drunk or angry these ranch hands got, they'd have to go back to the job sooner or later—to pick up their pay, if nothing else. Guillermo would get them at the camp and bore into them with a face that was built to look unfriendly—eyelids like mud, forehead like a wooden helmet, a scar that busted his left eyebrow in two. When he'd smack these guys, even the dumb ones never hit back.

In return, I'd help him patrol for cattle thieves—each of us cruising in our own trucks, or sometimes driving together to cut the boredom— patrolling to the edge of the land, doubling back where we'd just been, racing across to the other side, just trying to look like we were everywhere at once—sometimes hauling suspects back to our mail storage room, which was my holding cell. One time, it was as easy as following the cow scat. Those thieves hadn't even put the animal in a trailer. They just walked it onto the road, and we tracked them all the way to Pomona. Finally heard mooing from a tin warehouse, where I kicked in the door and we found a fat-faced teenaged cowhand named Michael and another one who'd also worked the ranch, Lon, whom I recognized from a crooked set of teeth that were the biggest thing on his face. They were cornered by a bleeding and angry heifer they'd tried to slaughter.

"This cow got in here!" Lon screamed when he recognized me.

"We don't know how he got in!" Michael said, his ear partly torn off. They had a large saw nearby and a knife— and newspapers, maybe to wrap the meat, maybe to catch the blood, maybe they didn't know.

I had my hand on my gun to shoot the animal, but Guillermo moved forward to calm it down. So I turned the gun to Lon and Michael, though obviously they wouldn't be going to jail right away. They'd be going to the hospital.

Guillermo believed in peculiar things. He would never leave his house on a Tuesday the 13th. He would never set anything on the floor, not even shopping bags. He would insist on telling me his nightmares, said it was important to talk about them as soon as they happened.

"I was in my father's house," Guillermo said as we sat in my truck, hidden in brush, fruitlessly watching a hole in the fence to see if the person who'd cut it would finally come around to take advantage of it. "But it didn't look like his house. And everything was dry. It was all this dry wood, and it cracked when I touched it. Then a door breaks, and a fire blows up, and everything's burning like weeds. And there's something really valuable. I forget what it is, but it seems really valuable, and I try to save it, and it burns into a black ball, like a tiny animal. And I wake up. But I don't know what burned."

"It was like an animal," I said.

"Yeah." We didn't say anything for a while, just stared at the fence. "How come you never tell me one of yours?" he asked.

I don't talk about my dreams, but it's not about luck—I don't know if I believe in any of that. It's just that my nightmares are boring. They're an anti-climax, after Guillermo's visions of lizard monsters and body parts floating down the river. My nightmares are always the same things. Like I'll be walking toward camp with my old army unit, and I realize I have to go back for something, and when I try to go to camp again, I can't find my unit and I can't find the camp and I walk and walk and never get there. Generally I walk until I wake up. Always like that—trying to go somewhere and never making it.

2.

Civilization hit Broken Hat in 1958, when the Uni-Mark Corporation bought about 80 square miles of grazing land. Four hundred acres of pasture—some of the greener grass in the area—were cleared flat like a runway, and the developers set about more or less instantly inventing a town.

From a distance, as I first saw them, the new houses looked like copies of a printed picture—as if this were still the early sketch of a town, with abstract, identical outlines of houses where the real ones would someday go. When Guillermo and I cruised through, the place felt like a ghost town in reverse. Dirt yards without trees or brush—what it might look like if mathematicians planned a human settlement. We stopped to look at a model home at the corner, with temporary furniture inside and a bright sign out front with the phone number for Uni-Mark Realtors. The air tasted of stucco and pastel paint.

"Who's gonna want to live here?" Guillermo said.

"The sheriff in Pomona says they're selling these hard out there."

"I got cousins in Chino. They never heard of it," he said. He worked the steel tip of his boot into the ground—an old instinct that something might be dug up. "My nephew could probably use a place out here."

"I don't know," I said. "I see myself creeping around here at night like a raccoon. Tipping over the garbage."

Over the next few months, the ranch hands hauled cows away without bringing back any new ones. For the sake of the realtors and the nice, new neighbors, the green, poison smell of cow shit slowly cleared away, leaving the scent of some light, native leaf I'd never noticed before—something young and hidden in the wind somewhere—an impossibly small aroma that would again be pushed out soon by the fumes of cars and barbecues and more construction.

As Guillermo's job started drying up from all this, he was promised more work at the Rankin Ranch in Chino. But he wouldn't be in charge—a step down, by any measure, even if the money eventually turned out as good. And truth be told, if Broken Hat was ranch land being broken up into identical dirt lots, Chino may not have been lagging far back. But Chino was about as far as Guillermo could go. Any time he changed houses, if he changed his schedule too much, his son would hurt himself.

"James Rankin is OK," Guillermo said. "I just keep my head down."

"You gotta save money."

"You don't have kids," he said. After a moment, he apologized. I said he didn't have to.

When the cattle hauling was done, Guillermo knocked on the front door of the sheriff's office and shook my hand. We made promises about going fishing some time. Then he drove off in his 1947 night-green Ford truck with the 10-year-old, countlessly retreaded tires, and a cattle trailer bearing two short, large-boned cows that no one else took.

Weeks later, the glint of silver moving vans—clusters of them, maybe three at a time. Driveways sprouted blue Chevy station wagons with tail fins as sharp as one of those miracle kitchen knives. Sometimes, from a distance, men in button-down plaid shirts and women in Dinah Shore dresses looked over at my station house, holding back small

6

children in short pants from across the former cattle pasture that separated us. But mostly they looked inward, toward their own homes and their neighbors.

Without much instruction coming to me from the county, I took it upon myself to patrol these new, bare streets. I told myself to resist my naturally unpleasant nature and just welcome these people to the neighborhood. I talked to one large-boned, cheerful woman named Raylene Dawson, who talked for a very long while about her husband's relatives in Sweden. I remember one man also came up and introduced himself without my prompting. That'd be Leonard Fahey. He was wiry, with a ducktail haircut. He wanted to know what kind of gun I carried.

It was a few weeks after people started moving into those undifferentiated new homes that I saw what pretended to be a police car—black-and-white, little red light on top. It was rolling down the newly created Mustang Drive, and I introduced myself to the other police department by pulling over their police vehicle with my police vehicle.

The driver had a close-cropped blond haircut like he was supposed to be military. But his face was soft and full. His suit was a checkered affair—a discount attempt at commanding legions—and his tie barely seemed to be holding him in.

He said his name was Dan Barsden. He said he was security supervisor for Uni-Mark. He said the company had its own security detail—and since apparently they could call it anything they wanted, they'd gone ahead and called it the Broken Hat Police Department.

"You patrol in a truck?" he said.

I told him it was going to be fun watching his boxy, piece-of-crap sedan get stuck in a dirt rut.

The county later told me the legality of this thing was hazy. But we would all just patrol the same area. Like brothers. We were the county, they were the "city"—except there was no "city," just unincorporated acreage with no independent government center, and no elected official overseeing the so-called city police. The only overseers would be Uni-Mark bosses, if they were even paying attention.

People who started living in the new places didn't care about a double-vision of patrol cars. Just seemed like an extra security feature for their immaculate new paradise. Most people figured Dan and I worked for the same department. I'd get a big wave whenever I cruised through, and kids would call out to me, "Sheriff Erik!" like it almost rhymed.

Dan's wife Rita started visiting everyone when they moved in—bringing them gifts, spreading gossip she'd picked up from visits elsewhere, and touring people's homes, even though all the houses had basically the same layout. After a month or two, her little Plymouth Valiant found its way down my dirt road, and she stepped out—a coiffed red-head who stood as straight as a fence picket, as if she had studied posture competitively.

"Well," she said, a little too loudly—projecting. "You live way out here!"

"It's kind of what I moved here for," I said.

"To be a hermit?"

"I work with people for a living. My career as a hermit was poorly thought out."

"Maybe you're fussy," she said, making me sound like a small dog.

She and Dan were having Fourth of July at their house, and she held monthly meetings where she and her friends talked about what they wanted this town to become, she said.

I was still getting used to the town how it was, and she was getting ready to change it.

"You seem ambitious," I said. "How did Dan ever drag you out here?"

She laughed. "I'm a good loyal wife." She mocked it while she said it. "Why didn't you ever get married?"

"The short answer is I don't know."

"What's the long answer?"

"The long answer is that I talk until we're both

8

uncomfortable, and I still don't know."

"You're dangerous," she said, which I obviously am not. She eventually got back in the Valiant, evenly pulled it around in a circle and followed the dirt road back out. I think that was the day I really knew the old ranch life was gone. This was her town, not mine.

Rita Barsden cooked everything ambitiously for July 4— a spaghetti dish that involved chicken liver, a chicken dish that involved veal bones. The aroma of garlic and meat fought with the new-house smell of fresh paint. While young couples tried making their toddlers eat the spaghetti, I drank whatever whiskey they had, and got stuck listening to a round, breathless man named Ronald Marks, who worked for a plumbing supply company two towns over.

"Got a weird letter at the office today," he told me. "We got the contract to supply pipe joints for the Granada development."

"Doesn't sound weird," I said. He was bragging, but I hadn't understood that yet. I can be a little slow.

Rita walked by in a yellow dress that looked like it was made partly from sunlight. "Everything is going great!" she said, touching me lightly on the collar as she breezed by. Dan sat by a kiddy pool, in short pants and a collared, button-down shirt, holding a highball like it was a theatrical prop.

There were more parties like this ahead in Broken Hat, more conversations with more Ronald Markses. I made an excuse that I had to patrol—and once I got in the truck and smelled the upholstery and cigarettes, I breathed a little better and held my head a little straighter. I made a left onto Mustang Drive with the windows rolled down and picked up speed, letting every piece of paper in the truck blow around free.

I cruised a couple hours looking for grass fires from the firecrackers, until I saw the Broken Hat Police car at Sioux Canyon Park parked next to a panel truck from the phone company. I guess Dan also found an excuse to leave the party. I pulled up crooked next to them on the dirt shoulder, stepped out into the dust and walked toward Dan and the phone company guy, both standing and looking up uselessly. A coyote was 22 feet in the air, tangled in the new telephone lines. It was like the ghosts of the old cowhands had come back to pull one more stupid, pointless stunt.

Dan abruptly ended his conversation with the phone guy and headed back to his car, while behind him, the animal was getting itself tangled up even worse and growling in all directions, vowing revenge on us all.

"So what's the plan?" I said.

The phone guy kind of looked down and said, "We've got to leave it up there for two days."

"Two days," I said. Dan kept walking.

"Uni-Mark has contracts with an animal control company and a crane company, and they're both going to take a couple of days," the phone guy said. "The coyote might be dead by then."

"Oh you think?" I inquired.

"The telephone lines are on Uni-Mark property," Barsden called back to me. "We're handling this."

"I'm relieved," I said. "Imagine how bad it'd be if you weren't."

"What?" he said.

"What?" I said.

Barsden got in his sedan and struggled away on the dirt road out of the gulch. I stood with the phone guy for a while. The coyote unloaded a wild stream of piss, which broke apart in the wind.

3.

Anne Lacraw was an anomaly in a town of young families—
a 50-ish woman living alone, in the same kind of three-
bedroom ranch home as everyone else. She would show up
at the local store every couple of days—sometimes viewing
you askew when you asked her something as simple as how
she was doing. I once saw her cut right in front of someone
in line and didn't even seem to be aware of it.

Then Kay—this kid who worked at the store and didn't
know she was supposed to reserve this sort of gossip for
Barsden—told me she hadn't seen Anne at the store in a
week. I cruised by Anne's place and saw her mail and
newspapers piling up in front of her house. When I
knocked, the door just pushed open. Everything in the
living room was upturned. Silverware and tax forms and old
power bills and sheets and broken dishes and books lay
piled up in the center.

The rest of the house was tidy, if a little dense. On the
walls hung framed pictures of people I didn't recognize, but
they held themselves like minor royalty. I counted at least
seven Bibles in various rooms, and Anne had ornate
candleholders around the kitchen. Her closet was thick with
sweaters and dresses and a single, perfectly clean and

pressed pair of overalls. One room was just for sewing, one just for reading. Everything was set in place, except in the living room, with this little Mount Baldy of garbage.

The neighbors closest to her house knew surprisingly little about her. Mrs. Davis next door said Anne mentioned having family nearby, but nobody had ever seen them. No one knew where she got her money. Apparently, I was the first person in town who'd even been in her house. None of the people I talked to asked me what it looked like inside.

Dan Barsden showed up later in a new patrol car on which Uni-Mark had painted a department motto— "Property, Life and Home"—making them sound like an insurance company. He pointedly did not look at me as I got back in my truck, and I guess he proceeded to go house to house, asking the same people the same questions I had.

4.

Meanwhile, I went straight to Leonard Fahey, who'd done carpentry work for Anne—and who, it was generally known, had burst out yelling and stormed off the job. Also, every pre-teen boy with nothing going on had started hanging around Leonard's house. Kids would spill out of the place fighting, or roll stolen shopping carts down the street with the younger kids riding inside, or see how close they could sneak up to the patrol truck, then retreat. Leonard's kind of charisma with children did not necessarily speak well for a man who was pushing 40.

Leonard's wife Carol gave me a little wave through the living room window as I pulled up. She had a chronic lung condition and spent most of her day sitting by the window, enjoying the sun. Leonard and some kids were around back at a picnic table, drinking out of paper cups.

"Looks like a party," I said, mostly to Leonard. The boys largely just looked down at the table, or off at the bare field behind Leonard's fence.

"They were playing a little street football," Leonard said, and addressed the kids. "Some of these guys got themselves scraped up pretty good." A couple of the boys smiled up for that. You could kind of tell who his favorite kids were, because they were the ones wearing their hair in a ducktail, same as his.

I told them I was going around the neighborhood checking with people about Anne Lacraw, to which Leonard innocently inquired, "Is she that older lady on Agua Mesa?"

"The one you screamed at, yes," I said. "Nobody's seen her for awhile. Looks like somebody tore through her house."

"I told her she ought to get a pack of dogs," he said, and he smoothed his hair back needlessly. "German Shepherds. They're thinkers. They stay loyal to one person. That's why the Nazis loved them."

"What was your argument with her?" I said.

"I know literally every dog in the neighborhood," he said, and the kids nodded.

"What was the argument?"

"It wasn't an argument. Women her age just go crazy when they live alone. Nothing was ever what she wanted."

"Was it about money?"

"No. It was just about her. Everything about her."

"My Dad helped Miss Lacraw unload her car," one kid piped in, "And a whole bag was just paper napkins." This was actually the most substantive thing I'd heard since arriving at Leonard's.

"She also used to hire that Mexican work crew," Leonard said, and he smoothed back his oiled hair again. "You talked to them?"

"I'm talking to everybody," I said.

"Too bad I wasn't at that break-in with my Luger. I was trained to fire at night."

"We'd have lost that war without you," I said, and a little while later I excused myself to go.

It was weirdly difficult to learn anything about Anne Lacraw. The agent at Emerald Realtors who sold her the house said the place was paid for in full with a cashier's check and didn't require a mortgage. When I went back to look at the house, Dan Barsden had nailed the front door shut, and he was in the front yard of Anne's house with a couple of bloodhounds—not a terrible idea. But the dogs just kind of circled around, not picking up anything.

"I heard you flipped your car out at Chaparral Park," I called out from my truck. "Why don't you get a truck before you kill yourself. And why does a grown man wear a clip-on tie?"

"If I get in a fight and somebody grabs my tie, it just comes off," he said.

By the end of that week, I'd accomplished nothing, except hauling in Leonard for giving alcohol to minors. A kid was weaving around on his bike after he left the Fahey house one afternoon. Ever make a drunk 11-year-old walk a straight line? You'll laugh until you die. Make him do it a couple times. Tell him he's getting better at it.

Inside, I found kids with paper cups again, drinking brandy and grape soda. Leonard deserved prison just for inventing that drink.

He said, "I'm gonna investigate how that alcohol got there," as I walked him out of the house and drove him to the "jail cell."

I heard the next day that Dan arrested Anne Lacraw's entire Mexican work crew.

5.

A second invasion of tract homes landed in the north hills, rising up even faster than this first landing of subdivisions. Meanwhile, some of the families who'd moved to Broken Hat only a couple of years earlier were already moving out. I also got lost on patrol because a house I'd unconsciously been using as a landmark had disappeared. Someone actually leveled this three-year-old structure, and replaced it with a home two-stories tall—the first multi-story building in town. That disappeared a little while later, too, because it was zoned wrong.

In February 1962—after having been governed offhandedly by the county all that time—Broken Hat became fully incorporated as a town. A week after that, I caught a 12-year-old boy named Terry at Broken Hat Elementary School at eight o'clock at night papering an entire wall with campaign posters, calling to elect Rita Barsden for town council. Terry started crying like I'd never seen any kid cry in my life—begging me not to tell his parents, of course, but also asking if I was going to take him to prison in Chino.

I didn't take him to his parents. I took him to the Barsden place. Rita greeted me at the door. The place was now a campaign headquarters, with kids in the living room folding fliers and stuffing envelopes. I told Rita that she could not put political materials on government-run property—and also that Terry needed to calm down.

"A lot of us never really did politics," Rita said. Her eyes blazed like in movies when people are dying of TB, or like in life when people try coffee for the first time. "It really sweeps you up. Would you ever want to run for office?"

"I have to go to county meetings sometimes," I said. "Sitting in a school auditorium 'til half past eleven, parsing everyone's non-problems. You can have it. It's more your town than mine."

"That's not true. Everyone belongs here."

"That can't be true," I said. "If everybody belonged in one place, anybody could live anywhere." I annoy people when I'm like this—when I twist everything around so it isn't good anymore.

People don't get real power by accident. Rita Barsden got in the paper a few days later. That took some doing, since the nearest newspaper was out in Pomona, and they weren't even going to cover our anthill election. But she got some reporter to drive out to here, and two days later, the paper published a slipshod little article about the lady candidate and Broken Hat's first taste of democracy. Plus, the reporter was kind of lazy. The only candidate he bothered quoting was Rita.

"Since people started moving out here," she said in print, "We've learned how to make old friends quickly."

Good line. Probably wrote it in advance. Good for her, making it sound natural.

6.

After I arrested Leonard, he decided we were great friends, and he started inviting me over and telling me ridiculous stories. Here's one about his family.

"My great-grandfather prevented the great massacre of Bad Water Canyon—which you never heard about because it didn't end up happening.

"Now he was coming west in a covered wagon. Great-grandpa said he had to drink out of the same bowl as the mules. And they stop at Bad Water Canyon, but they can tell something's up because they saw three butterflies on a flower—which is bad luck. And there's no birds. So they're just trying to get the animals fed, when you see puffs of dust on the horizon, and Geronimo rumbles in with a band of warrior braves."

Let me just stop and point out: this part of the story is certifiably false. Geronimo raised all his hell in the Southwest, trying to kill Mexico. The Oregon Trail would have been too far north to matter. It could conceivably have been Sitting Bull. But let's be blunt. It wasn't him, either. It wasn't anybody.

"The Indians whooped and hollered and galloped around them for eighteen days and nights. Then one morning, my great grandfather gets a little dust in his glass eye, pops it out and sticks it in his mouth to clean it. Well this little Indian girl sees it and just shrieks and runs for her ma."

And what's a little Indian girl doing with a war band? This wasn't an attack. The Indians were probably just traveling along with the wagons, likely begging for cigarettes. If this happened at all. Which it didn't.

"Well that's when the Indians retreat. And they hang back until Geronimo himself walks forward..."

...which, as I said, Geronimo did not do...

"...because Geronimo was born without fear. And Geronimo says, 'They tell me you eat your own eye for breakfast.'

"And gramps says, 'I grow a new one every morning.' He pops his eye out again and hands it to the great chief, and says, 'Try it yourself.' Well, the great chief puts the glass eye in his mouth and breaks his teeth on it.

"Gramps says, 'Ain't it delicious.'

"And Geronimo won't admit he's beat. So he looks at great grandpa straight on, swallows that glass eye whole, and says, 'Thank you for the eye. Now you go in peace.'

He gathers up his men, and they start to ride away. But just before they disappear, Geronimo turns to great-granddad one more time and says, 'Wherever you go, I will see what you see.'

And gramps says, 'Yeah. But you'll see out your butt.'"

Rita won the election, of course. She got the second-most votes for one of the three council seats—the first female council member in the county. I didn't vote for her, of course. But I didn't vote for anyone. Why would I? This wasn't a real town. So it didn't have a real council. Who cared?

7.

Rev. David Makinaw was showing me around the United Church of Christ in Pomona, which is where Anne Lacraw's calendar had come from. The church was still a relatively new building, with everything painted white. The congregation had been renting space at the old mission until five years ago.

"She was a regular, though, right?" I asked him.

"That's a mild way of putting it. Just don't sit in her usual pew," the reverend said—sort of smiling, but serious on this point. He showed me a seat near the back of the church, near the center of the row—as if the mere sight of it had a chance of actually clearing up something. "A child sat there once, and she went charging at him—just yelling at him, even though he was running away. Nobody's sat there since, even while she's gone."

"Was anybody mad at her here?"

"No, not mad. A little...put off for a while. She's sweet as pound cake some of the time. I think she even got cookies for the boy later, like nothing happened. Did she ever report the thefts?"

"Thefts? No. What thefts?"

"Little things around the house. Some money, clothing. I

told her to call the police." He shrugged.

"Who's her doctor?" I asked. The reverend seemed confused by the question, and said he didn't know that either.

"Any reason this pew is special?" I said. "Who sat next to her?"

"Well, sometimes Mrs. Avery, sometimes not. Sometimes Mr. Beachum is in front of her."

I sat down in Anne's place, and the reverend actually looked a little nervous. But if she suddenly jumped out screaming, at least we'd know where she was.

The seat was near the middle of the row. Probably no one would have to climb past her to reach a seat—always just easier to come from one side of the aisle or the other. Right in the center, seeing everything, not having to stand for anyone.

"Sounds like she was already coming here before she moved to Broken Hat," I said. "Where did she live when she joined the church?"

"Well, I believe all the Lacraws used to live on Lacraw Road. By the orange groves."

"Ah. So that's not a coincidence. Did her family buy her that house?"

"I don't know. But her cousins are the Campbells. So."

"As in the Campbells."

"The Lacraws were the less wealthy relations," the reverend said.

Inasmuch as the town had any local legend, this was it: back in the 1920s, Mrs. Campbell fainted in the kitchen of the Campbell mansion while her husband was cutting vegetables—and thus had a knife in his hand. When he bent over to help her, the maid came in and saw the master clutching a knife and bending over the fallen mistress. So the maid stabbed him to death.

Guillermo and I used to pick out everything wrong with that story—why the maid would have instantly made that assumption, why he was cutting up vegetables in the first place if he had a maid for that sort of thing, and most of all, how hard it is to kill anyone quickly with a knife unless you know exactly what you're doing.

When I got back from the church, I found Dan Barsden sitting in his car outside my office. He just nodded, waved me on like I needed to get out of his way.

I found a notice taped to the front door, saying the sheriff's office building and the land underneath it had been purchased by the Uni-Mark corporation. I would have to vacate the office within thirty days.

So Dan was just here to see my reaction. Say that about him—the personal touch. I knocked on his car window.

"Having a nice time here, Dan?" I said.

"It wasn't my idea," he said.

"Don't worry about me, Dan. I don't need an office. Strip me down to my skivvies, I'm still Sheriff."

"You know, you could work for Uni-Mark."

"You looked like you were having fun with those bloodhounds the other day. Didn't your mom ever let you have pets when you were a kid?"

"Seriously. They've got security posts all over the county. I've told them about you."

"You can't just get dogs from the pound for that kind of thing."

"They're from a breeder in Chino. Just ask where I got the dogs, if that's what you want. I want to help you, Eric."

"Congratulations to your wife for everything she's accomplishing here."

"This isn't her either, Eric."

"Hey. I'm complimenting her. This is really well done."

"Why do you have to turn this into a fight when it doesn't have to be a fight."

"You seem tense. You want an aspirin?"

"Go kill yourself, Eric."

His wheels spit dust as he took off.

As a practical matter, what difference would it make whether I worked for Uni-Mark or not? Do I love the county government so much? It's just that Uni-Mark comes in and makes up a town, like it's a real thing and we're all supposed to believe in it. Guillermo and I shaped the old ranch. We understood all those guys. We wore down the roads. Then Uni-Mark takes the old Route 6 and the starts calling it Mustang Way, like that's actually what it is—like we ever even used mustangs on the ranch. And the people who move in just write it on their envelopes like it's the truth, like it isn't some commercial affectation. These streets—these duplicate homes—they feel like the most sickening compromise. The houses don't even really belong to the people in them. This is Uni-Mark's imitation of a town.

I think a lot about geography. I memorize state capitals, and I stare for hours at maps of the world. I think if you live someplace for a while, part of you sort of always stays—even if you didn't like it there. I think if you travel too much, you become a collection of scattered referents that no one else shares—like a book in a dead language, or a map to things that picked up and went somewhere else.

Now, suppose your mind starts shrinking, and the world doesn't total up anymore. You starve down to a few memories, a few thoughts you trust. People will find you staring at a balloon or reciting some old story or wearing ice skates on the curb of a hot street. Older people who start losing their minds—they forget things. They forget they yelled at some kid in church. Or they forget they gave away a ring, or that they moved it from its usual spot. So they think someone stole it. Or they tear up the house looking for something, leaving everything in a pile. And eventually, their only compasses are simple, childish instincts from a dead era. But even so, even if you lose everything else, if you grew up in an orange grove, wouldn't that still matter? Wouldn't you find some comfort in the aroma of orange blossoms, without necessarily even knowing the reason?

The orange groves on Lacraw Road were maybe a mile north of the Broken Hat utility station—the perfume from them still reached town when the wind blew south. The bloodhounds barked like desperate howler monkeys as I drove them up there from Chino, because dogs also have to figure out a place. And then, of course, the smell of oranges

24

confused them, just overwhelming everything else. We went from one spot to the next, trying to pick up Anne's scent, until one of the dogs nosed where, frankly, I should have looked first—the old Campbell house, a two-story Spanish mansion covered with weeds and ruin, without a single un-busted window in the front. I knocked on the door, with all my bellowing hounds, and Ann Lacraw answered it wearing a blue formal dress that she'd wearing for days—stained with dirt and sweat and orange juice. She looked half starved, probably living on old canned food and whatever still grew in the grove, maybe forgetting to eat altogether sometimes.

"I want my bath," she ordered—which actually did seem like the best plan all around.

8.

I couldn't leave Anne alone at her house, and I still couldn't find any family for her, so she stayed at my ranch. She was barely settled before she began passionately whining on my behalf that I deserved an office.

"People need to pay respect," she said. "They don't have that kind of power. This is our home. You built the whole town. How can they do a thing like this to you?"

While I did sort of help build the town, she had no way of knowing that, and I sensed she may have thought she was talking to someone else. "It doesn't have to be fair," I said. She kept harping on about it—until minutes later when she apparently forget the entire topic. By then, she seemed to presume she owned my house, and asked why the workers had left the side yard such a mess.

"We need to move that tree," she said. "Someone was supposed to replant that tree."

I took her on patrol with me, and she wasn't bad company, in a way—pointing at houses and asking if I could imagine living there.

"I don't see the difference between most of these places," I said.

"Look at that house," she said, pointing to a place in the

27

middle of the block where they'd installed a gate and over-planted the yard—as thick as virgin jungle. That family didn't end up living there too long. The husband worked at a college or something. "Those are hollyhocks. That's a fried-egg flower. That's going to be a sycamore—that sapling. And those are Calliopsis."

She said a lot of people were stupid with their houses, which got me wondering how she judged my house.

But then she'd get tired and confused. About an hour later, when I stopped some kids who were playing with firecrackers, she rushed out of my truck, yelling at them.

"Get out of here!" she said, as if the street were her property. "Nobody invited you here! Get out!" She said it over and over, as if her voice had the power of some natural force. The kids stood staring at her, too distracted by the spectacle to run for safety.

Then there was the way she treated Carol Fahey. The town invalid had actually left her living room and driven Leonard's camper truck down the dirt road to my house, bringing fresh makeup for Anne, and a casserole made from canned meat. Anne repaid this surprising courtesy by treating Mrs. Fahey like the help. Anne told her the makeup looked cheap. She criticized the way Carol sat, the way she drank her coffee. At one point, she handed Carol my coat and told her to hang it up—and Carol Fahey, who'd barely been off the couch since I'd known her, went off in search of the closet, smiling in the face of a seemingly perilous task.

I counted on Anne at least being equally rude to Dan and Rita Barsden when they came by the next day. But you'd have thought Rita was Jackie Kennedy.

"Please pardon the mess," Anne told her as they came in. "No one's come to trim the side yard."

"We just wanted to check on your welfare," Rita said.

"Well, you know, so many of the wrong kind of people have been coming around. Things disappear. We all know who's responsible."

"The Mexicans?" Dan said.

"Leona Shannessy," Anne practically whispered. None of us knew who that was. Maybe someone she remembered from a long time ago.

"And have you been eating all right?" Rita said. Anne would barely eat anything I gave her. I'd fry her a steak, some potatoes, open a can of vegetables, and she'd just pick at it. Then she'd eat cookies all night, like a kid.

"I don't want to get too fat," Anne said. "Like Fatty Patty!" And she laughed.

Rita smiled, since that seemed to be required. I had to respect this visit. She'd already won the election. She didn't need votes.

Dan kept trying to pry details from Anne about her Mexican crew. But that didn't interest Anne at all. Things either interested her right away, or never. She did not change her mind. After a while, Dan and I found ourselves sitting like sandbags while Anne and Rita studied a magazine that Rita brought.

"You could dress like that," Anne told Rita. "That's what the actresses wear now." She wanted to dress Rita Barsden right there.

But after awhile, she was acting a little giddy, clingy—and calling Rita "Helen," even after she was corrected a couple of times.

Rita pulled me aside on her way out. "This is a very good thing you're doing," she said. "It's not nice when she's running around like that."

Then the Barsdens headed out. Anne stood on the porch watching their retreating dust down my road.

"Everyone loves her," she finally said. "It never changes. All their friends are waiting for them." I couldn't tell if she really meant Rita, or if she was talking about something from the 1930s.

Anne was back on her good behavior the next day at the Hall of Records—just sat at the table like school was in session, while I flipped through real estate records trying to figure out who the original purchaser was for her house. I finally had to go up to the County Clerk—a tidy, bow-tied man named Melvin Fremont, who looked like an official photograph of himself.

"Who looked at the records recently?" I asked.

"I'm afraid all our sign-in sheets from this year are missing," he said. "We're not happy about it."

"My condolences."

"We just bury them in storage at the end of the year anyway, but this one is gone already—this giant binder."

"Any idea why there's a property missing here?"

"I'm sorry?"

"See the older lady over there? She lives at 109 Agua Mesa in Broken Hat. But in the deeds, and there's nothing between 107 Agua Mesa and 111."

Melvin calmly informed me that's not possible, then went over and looked at the deed files, then looked at the map, then at the deed files, then at the map, and so on. Occasionally I thought he might stop, but then he'd keep going.

"I am going to get this straight," he finally said. He looked like he'd come to school without his homework. "When you come back, this will be straight."

When I went back to the table, I whispered to Anne, "Who in your family bought your house? Do you remember?"

Anne looked around the room, respecting the silence, then said very carefully, "Great granddaddy built it all by himself, in 1873."

"No, not the house where you grew up. I mean the house on Agua Mesa," I said. "Do you know where that one came from?"

"Our family owns that land," she said.

"So your family bought the house for you?"

"It's their land." She seemed to be losing patience with me.

Actually, it was Uni-Mark's land. I ended the workday phoning in yet another message to the company—this time asking if they had any idea who'd bought Anne's house for her. By now, I'd made a habit of tracking down every corporate officer at Uni-Mark and leaving messages on every topic. Once, to be funny, I left a message for their vice president of acquisitions, saying, "Ask him if he knows the circumference of the sun." That prank felt hollow even to me.

When I finally did get my first communication from the company—days after my trip to the county seat—it was a subpoena. I was to give a deposition as material witness against Anne's old Mexican work crew—Angelo Galvan, "Michael Smith" and Jaime Latigua. They were still being charged with her disappearance, even though I found her. I left new messages asking exactly what crime these men had committed, given that Anne had wandered off on her own and probably trashed her own house. As usual, I heard nothing. Even old Dan Barsden himself hadn't been cruising around much lately.

I was also well along asking the county when they'd replace my old office. Using my house for headquarters was going to become mighty awkward if I had to lock up some drunk for the night—especially with Anne there, asking the detainee whether he knew "Helen," or why he hadn't cleaned up the yard.

But since the county wasn't paying much attention to me anyway, at least it was easy to visit Angelo, "Michael" and Jaime—the official suspects in the disappearance of a woman who was no longer missing. Flash your badge and they let you right into county lock-up, while Anne sat there with a guard who ended up getting ordered around by her and having to get her lunch.

In the holding cell, the four suspects looked at me like I'd invaded their homes.

"We did not do nothing," said a small older man with lines on the backs of his hand, after I asked what the charges against them were. He turned out to be Jaime Latigua.

"Yes, but what did they say you did?"

"We did not do nothing," Jaime Latigua said again.

"They say we scared the lady. They said we steal," Angelo Galvan said. We recognized each other. He had worked at the old Broken Hat Ranch. "We don't steal."

Michael Smith sat in the corner staring at me like a cat that thinks it's invisible as long as it doesn't move. He was young, maybe a teenager, probably from the countryside. I suspected it was an ordeal just leaving his home town for other parts of Mexico, let alone coming to a different country altogether. I also suspected the only two words he knew in English were Michael and Smith.

Angelo said he and Michael and Jaime were brothers, even though they had different last names and they didn't look alike, and at least 30 years obviously separated Michael and Jaime. I let it go.

"So did you scare the lady?"

"No," Angelo said. "Someone else. She always say someone is poisoning her."

"We do not poison her," Jaime said. I think he was struggling to be the leader of the group.

"OK," I said.

"But she say things that I do not understand," Angelo said.

"Crazy things," I said.

Angelo smiled. "You say that word. That is your word."

"Yeah. It's my word. What kind of things did she say?"

"She makes us plant trees in the backyard. Then we come back, and the trees are in different places. And she says we do it."

"Think she was out there at midnight moving those trees around by herself?"

"She could."

"Did she say who was poisoning her?"

"She just says they give her drugs and make her crazy, and someone is trying to control her. You ask her. They say she is talking."

"Sort of. Who said she's talking?"

"Policia. She says we rob her and we scare her."

"We do not rob her," Jaime said.

"The police said she said that? Is that what they told you?"

"Yes."

"That's funny," I said.

"That is funny?" Angelo said. "It must be a different kind of humor."

"Yes," I said. "It's hilarious."

Within twenty-four hours, Dan Barsden skidded up in front of my ranch house in a Pontiac Grand Prix—the fourth new patrol car he'd driven in the relatively short time I'd known him.

"What are you doing?" he asked.

"Dan. How've you been? You losing weight?"

Dust still hung from his arrival, and settled on his boots. At least he'd finally learned how to dress for a dirt road.

"Why are you tampering with my evidence?" he said. "I could have you arrested. I'm not—out of professional courtesy. But why don't I get courtesy in return?"

"What are you talking about? What evidence?"

"You told my suspects that Anne didn't implicate them."

"I," I said carefully, "did not tell them that."

"Bullshit. I go there this morning, and suddenly they're all confident, and saying she didn't accuse them of anything."

"She didn't."

"That's because she's confused. She doesn't know anything."

"Not true. She knows what the weather was like in the 1920s."

"You're no longer allowed to talk to my suspects."

"What are you doing, Dan? You have three guys in jail. Why?"

"This is not your business."

"Who bought Anne a house?"

"What is it with you and her house? Did you hear what I just said, Eric?"

"Who bought Anne Lacraw a house?"

"Did you hear what I said?"

"Yeah. Who bought Anne's house?"

"What did I just say?"

"You said you're an asshole. Now Anne told people at her church somebody bought her a house. Uni-Mark won't

33

tell me who they dealt with."

"What this is, is it's not your business."

"I am the sheriff. It is my business when somebody gets arrested. Who bought Anne Lacraw's house?"

"Probably Anne Lacraw bought Anne Lacraw's house."

"And somebody stole her property records. Why'd that happen?"

The anger in his face flickered uncertainly for a moment.

"You know the Mexicans did something," he finally said. "And none of them have papers."

"If you want to get them on immigration, get them on immigration. But what is this?"

"Don't talk to them," he said. "Don't talk to them. I don't want to repeat myself."

"You don't?"

"Don't talk to them," he repeated.

He drove off. More dust.

9.

When it was time to go to the court hearing for Angelo Galvan, Jaime Latigua and "Michael Smith," Anne got herself together in every detail, like she was going to church—mousey, graying hair pulled back, shoes shined, the sort of Florentine hat that I vaguely remembered from the 1930s.

We ended up in the second row of the gallery—she, the ostensible victim of this purported crime, and I, the officer who found her. Despite his yellow tie, gray coat and slicked back hair, the prosecutor looked like a shoe salesman who was just a little too old to be in the game anymore. Dan Barsden sat next to him, with his hands folded on the prosecution table, staring ahead like he was doing something useful. The judge was old Norm Coolidge, who normally handled traffic matters, and had already tried retiring twice, but still hadn't been replaced.

Over at the defense table sat Angelo, Jaime and "Michael." They were on their own.

Nobody in the courtroom looked like they wanted to be there—except Jaime, who seemed determined, and Angelo, who looked oddly comfortable.

The prosecutor got up and read the indictment—that Mr. Galvan, Mr. Latigua and Mr. Smith were Mexican and

Honduran nationals working in the town of Broken Hat on or about 1962 and 1963. That they performed assorted maintenance tasks for Anne Lacraw, age 55. That such-and-such a law forbids harassment. That the three men engaged in a campaign of harassment. That when Miss Lacraw fled the premises due to this intimidation, the defendants burglarized and despoiled her premises, in order to remove some still-undetermined valuables.

The prosecutor then brought Dan to the stand, who testified that he had seen the defendants working for Lacraw. He described what her house looked like after she disappeared—how it seemed to have been ransacked. He then told them my report of where I'd found her hiding.

"Can you think of any other reason why Miss Lacraw might have fled her house?"

"No," Dan said.

They showed some pictures. They showed some maps. Then the prosecution rested. Damnedest thing I'd even seen. They had nothing. They didn't even call the victim to the stand. They didn't even call me.

The judge turned to the defense and said, "The court and the prosecutors show Jaime Latigua as representing the defense."

Nice move. Hand the lead job to Jaime—the older guy, who thought he knew more than he really did. They flattered him, made him think he deserved the leadership role by virtue of seniority. Only way to make it worse is if they'd handed the job to Michael Smith.

"Judge, sir," Jaime said, "we do not do these things. We do not steal. We are honest." He went on that way for a while until the judge asked this man with limited English skills if he had any evidence.

But if the prosecutor could flatter Jaime's vanity, so could Angelo. The young man handed his elder a note, letting him know that although the elder was in charge, perhaps this humble item might be of some service.

"I call to the stand Anne Lacraw."

36

Anne walked up to the stand as if being called for jury duty rather than testimony. When the clerk swore her in, her lips followed the oath along with him.

Then Jaime asked, "Misses Lacraw, d0 we do these things? D0 we steal? D0 we hurt you?"

Anne leaned forward and enunciated very clearly for the court, "I don't know. Why are you asking me this?"

That kind of stumped everybody for a bit. Jaime wandered back to the table for some clue what to do next. Angelo handed him another small piece of paper.

"Misses Lacraw," Jaime said. "What happened the day you left your home for the orange grove?"

"When I went to the orange grove?"

"Yes."

"Why does that matter? I lost my necklace."

Another piece of paper from Angelo. Jaime looked at the piece of paper. He looked at Angelo, then at the piece of paper. Then he asked, "Misses Lacraw, what year is it?"

She was halfway into answering—I was anticipating early in FDR's presidency— when the prosecutor shouted over her.

"Objection your honor. Trivial and irrelevant."

Angelo didn't have the legal language to defend the question. So the objection stood. After Jaime talked in circles with her awhile more, it was obvious she had no clear complaint against the defendants. She barely remembered them at all. After straining to find more to ask about, Jaime finally said he had no more questions, and walked back to the defendant's table.

The prosecutor got up.

"Miss Lacraw, you mentioned losing a necklace?"

"Yes. It was a blue necklace that my father gave me. I always kept it in the drawer of the sewing room. Daddy said he bought it from a special store all the way in the city—a real jewelry store."

"So you rushed out of the house to find it. You were driven out of the house—to find a precious family heirloom."

"I looked for Daddy in the orange groves. I was out so late."

"And how much was the necklace worth?"

"I don't know," she said. Then turned to me. "Daddy," she asked, "How much was the necklace?"

I am, if anything, a little younger than Anne. The prosecutor, the judge, Dan Barsden and Angelo looked over at me. I nodded slightly, a fair-weather greeting to them all.

After court let out for recess, I found Dan Barsden outside, smoking a menthol cigarette and looking like a kid at Thanksgiving who'd been kicked out of the grown-up's table.

"Well, I think we all learned something today," I said.

He was not in the mood. I'd picked the worst moment in his life to approach him—which, believe it or not, had not occurred to me until that moment.

"Listen Dan," I said. "Is that job at Uni-Mark still on the table?"

"What do you want, Eric?"

"I'm serious. I'm going to need a job," I said. "Handwriting is on the wall. The county won't tell me when I'll get a new office. Hell, they won't say anything. This may surprise you, Dan—because God knows, you don't deserve it—but things are trending your way. They have been for a while."

He stared at me for a bit. "I'll talk to some people," he finally said. "What do you want me to tell them?"

"Tell them I could've done a better job setting up that work crew."

He took a drag on that fucking menthol cigarette, and exhaled through his nose. "I'm going to miss you Eric."

"Just tell them I'm gonna lose my job," I said, "Though I suppose they already know that, and you've probably told them everything else about me."

"You think you're that important?" he said. Ah, the old Dan was back. It actually felt kind of good that I made the man's lousy day slightly better.

10.

At some point, in a flurry of patriotism, the town of Broken Hat decided it would be a tremendous idea to have a Boy Scout troop. Most people were too busy to run it, of course. But fortunately—inevitably—Leonard Fahey actually wanted the job. He received the town's appointment as scoutmaster, and started carting the boys around to camping trips, volunteer activities, jamborees and other things that parents liked bragging about. Leonard became a prominent figure in town.

One of the drawbacks to working alone the way I did was that I couldn't make little side bets with co-workers. In this case, it might have been fun to put money on the exact time and date when Leonard would finally drive a van full of kids off the road.

If you'd chosen May 16, 1964, at around 9:05 p.m., you'd have won that office pool.

One kid broke his arm. Leonard was a little drunk, of course, as were a couple of the boys. But more interesting than that, when I went through the process of getting his driving privileges suspended, his license turned out to be false. No record of him at the DMV at all. Also, for all his talk about the war, I couldn't scare up any military records. Altogether, there was no trace of him before he and Carol got married up San Bernardino County.

For about two minutes, I actually wondered if he was a Soviet agent. We had aerospace industry nearby, and he was just the kind of idiot no one would suspect. But then it seemed to me the Soviets would've done a better job contriving a background for him.

Carol Fahey and their son Evan had only ever known him as Leonard. As for the man himself, his explanation was in character.

"Yeah, you're not going to find any military records," he said comfortably. "They're not supposed to keep records for the kind of thing I did. We hashed it out with President Eisenhower. That's why I got special dispensation for the driver's license."

"So if I reach President Eisenhower, he'll clear this up."

"He can't," Leonard said. "You don't have that kind of security clearance. All I'm authorized to say is, there's a reason the Nazis never invaded Kenya."

There was basically nothing else to discuss. I charged him for the fake license and the reckless driving, but he hadn't stolen anything. He'd even bought his house in cash, so I didn't find a mortgage agreement under a suspect name. You can't arrest a man just for having no past.

The Barsdens agreed to keep an eye on Anne while I went for my job interview at Uni-Mark. I thought Anne would be thrilled, but she seemed frightened. She must have changed her clothes six times before we drove over there, and she approached Rita Barsden with careful rehearsed steps, as if this were a test. Dan, in the meantime, looked like he was already a little sick of Anne before she even showed up.

My interview was an hour-and-a-half away in Los Angeles. Well, actually an hour away—the roads were smoother since I last drove there. I ultimately got funneled onto the new freeway, where my truck made me look like Pa Fetchit heading into the city for his annual bath. If I allowed myself to relax, cars would suddenly merge into my lane from random directions. Little lunchbox houses clustered more thickly as I drove west, and I didn't exactly arrive in the city, more like I slipped into it imperceptibly, the dusty buildings haltingly getting bigger and closer together, and the orange groves thinning away to nothing.

Uni-Mark's branch office on Wilshire Boulevard was small but polished. Everything felt new—the smell of new carpeting, unseasonably cool air on the back of my neck. This was maybe the second or third time I'd ever experienced air conditioning, and it felt like we were all being kept fresh in the vegetable bin.

A woman with a slight but impressive resemblance to Kim Novak smiled professionally and directed me to the office of Ronald St. Clair, vice president of operations—a short, trim man with a surprisingly strong handshake.

"I appreciate your driving out here," Vice President Ron said. "I'd likely get lost driving out your way."

"No you wouldn't, but I appreciate the modesty," I said.

"It's nice to be appreciated," he said. "So how much do you know about Uni-Mark?"

"Your main office is in San Mateo. You laid down housing developments in five different counties in California and two in Oregon. You tend to plant them along the routes of future highways."

"You know our secret recipe."

"Sherman Campbell here today?"

"No. Mr. Campbell works out of a different office."

"His home, I'm guessing. He is one of the Campbells."

"He does have deep roots in your community, yes."

"I imagine he's also kind of a pain in the ass."

"That's one of my colleagues you're talking about, Mr. Mulliner."

"Is he?" I said. "You graduated Stanford with a degree in business, Ron, and you've been working your way up in development companies for fifteen years. But Sherman Campbell—he got a position with Uni-Mark shortly after you guys started developing his land. Land he inherited."

"I am at least impressed with your research."

"Don't give me too much credit. It's mostly the byproduct of trying to chase down everyone in this company for the last few months. Campbell's name kind of jumped out."

"And you're disappointed I'm not him."

"No offense. It's just that—meeting you—I can't imagine you care one way or another if three Mexican landscapers get convicted in court."

"Broken Hat reflects on Uni-Mark," he said, with an excellent poker face. "I want it to be a nice town."

"Yeah, but this is something else. Somebody really wants to prove Anne Lacraw didn't just wander off on her own. And somebody bought her a house. I don't think a nice business school graduate with actual responsibilities in this company would sweat that kind of detail. But a distant relative who happens to be an officer in the firm..." I let that trail off to see if he'd fill in the gap—to see if a long silence made him uncomfortable. It didn't. He watched me as if he were carefully studying a bird.

"Well," I finally concluded, "Don't blame Dan Barsden for my behavior."

"I did read your messages, Sheriff Mulliner. I kind of suspected what was coming," he said. He left a long pause— maybe to see if it made me uncomfortable enough to say more. Finally, he said, "If you ever actually did want a job with us, what sort of town would you want to live in?"

I hadn't really thought about that, and I sat looking like an idiot for a moment. I hate job interview questions I don't expect. "Well—when I went to Broken Hat, I knew I could buy a little farm and tool around on the ranch. That's kind of what I signed up for."

"We've got a few planned farmed communities in the design stage."

"You can plan a farm town?"

"You can plan anything. We're looking at places in the Central Valley. Small farms are consolidating, so it's not really going to be farm families anymore. They'll need housing for skilled labor, support services, infrastructure. Do you mind the smell of cows?"

"I actually miss it."

"Well. When you're honestly ready, and when you're not just coming around with ulterior motives, you have our number and all our names."

He gave me that steel handshake again, and said, "2.7 million miles."

"Pardon?"

"The circumference of the sun. You left a message asking about it. You got me curious. It's 2.7 million miles."

Kim Novak bid me an efficient goodbye. The building lobby was shiny and indifferent, and the hot air blasted my eyes when I opened the door to the street. I bought something called a pastrami sandwich, which was very salty and very good, and made me feel more full than expected. My truck squeaked as I climbed back in, and I rattled back onto the super highway.

11.

When I finally got a call from old Melvin at the records office, he still didn't have the deed to Anne's house, but he also didn't have the deed to three other places: two houses on La Barranca Way and the one little store in town, over by Silver Water Street. A few days later he called me up again to say he was missing two more deeds—and he knew for a fact he had just seen them the week before. The world was disappearing under Melvin's feet. I, in the meantime, had no idea why Uni-Mark would take these other records. And I would never know. I had given up.

Another funny thing that same week: about two hundred head of cattle ambled onto the level path the road crews had cleared for the Interstate when it would cut through town someday. Maybe these animals had been living like nomads in the hills all this time. But for whatever reason, no one laid claim to them, as they knocked over equipment and ruined survey lines.

It had been years since we had any real cattlemen nearby. We had to truck some in from San Bernardino County and pull a few gimps out of retirement. And there was Guillermo Calderon, the cut in his eyebrow now more deeply embedded and resolved as he ordered his crew around. It'd been so long since I'd seen him, I'd started to think I'd only imagined him.

"Eric," he said. "Why are you still here?"

"Waiting for Hollywood to call," I said. "So what do you do all day now?"

"I fix things in my house. Then I break 'em again," he said without smiling. "If I weren't so old, I'd be trying to pick fights." He looked around at the ranch hands. "I might flick one of these guys in the nose."

I vaguely remembered some of the men who were now chasing after these cows—and I definitely remembered these same kinds of stupid conversations—the same rage at anyone they perceived as being slightly dumber than themselves. Over on a horse was Michael, who'd walked a cow from Broken Hat to Pomona so long ago. Michael's face was fatter than I remembered. I didn't see his old partner Lon anywhere nearby, and Michael looked like he was having a little trouble staying balanced on the saddle. He was always talentless—but still, I didn't remember him being this bad.

It was a long day, during which I told Guillermo I was trying to reach any of the Campbells. Where did they even live anymore?

"I don't know them, either," he said. "I used to know the servants, but I think a bunch of them went back to Mexico. Maybe their kids are still around." He was thinking about something else. "Didn't there used to be a hill over there?"

"You're looking east. You got yourself turned around," I said.

"Oh," he said. "Yeah. The markings are all different."

"It kind of breaks my heart a little, seeing you get lost."

"It's a good thing you're not around me anymore. I can't even sleep at night. I just cruise around in my truck. Sometimes I'll drive onto other people's land, with my headlights shut off. I'm gonna get myself shot."

"Sounds like it."

"You should come with me some time. We'd look

hilarious, dying like that."

"Well, I'm weighing a lot of career options. But that one is now currently in the lead."

12.

Pilar Cortez apparently saved up so much money working for the Campbells that she set up her daughter Lena with her own small hotel in Pomona. I found Lena Cortez serving a bland but reliable lunch for the early crowd in the hotel restaurant. Though I introduced myself as the sheriff and said I was there on business, she seated Anne and me like just two more guests—placing a pitcher of water and a basket of white bread in front of us before making one last pass through the rest of the dining area to ensure things were running how she liked.

Anne looked unusually comfortable, though she didn't touch the bread.

Lena sat down with us after some delay, but completely present, totally ours.

"I'm working a pretty tenuous connection here," I told her. "I'm trying to find some family for this lady. Her cousins are the Campbells. I know your mom worked for them, but do you have any way of reaching any of them?"

"I'm sorry. Once Mama went back to Mexico, the Campbells and I had no reason to call each other."

"Do they ever contact your mom?" I said.

"No," Lena said. "Once she was done, she was done."

"Is she doing all right?"

"She's very rich there. She has a big ranch—as big as the Campbells' ranch, actually. She saved every dime. It was a shock to me. We were always poor when I was a kid, and when she bought me this place, I felt so bad, like she handed me everything. But then she went down south and became like a land baron."

"Neat plan."

"I think her plan was to stay and help me run this place."

"Why didn't she?"

She turned to Anne. "Would the lady like a vanilla Coke?"

"Oh yes," Anne said. "Daddy always made those."

"Sure." Lena turned back to me. "Come watch me make a vanilla Coke. It's a skill. Everybody should learn it." I probably looked a little reluctant. "The staff will take care of the lady. They know what's what."

I followed her to the hotel bar—which didn't really look like a bar, more like a front desk. But it had bottles and an icebox and spices and syrups on a high shelf.

"There's a lot I can't say in front of your friend," she said. "The Campbells had my Mom deported."

"Why would they do that?"

"She saw too much in the crazy house. It's another thing they did just all a sudden, like always."

"Did your mother witness the stabbing?"

"No. But it didn't surprise her. Didn't surprise anybody. Mr. Campbell used to go into a rage—just for nothing. I don't want to be rude, but does your friend have any mental problems?"

"She's about fifty-fifty on calling me by the right name."

"They all got crazy like that. One time, Mr. Campbell was digging a trench—with three guys, he was digging a trench—and like, out of nowhere, he looks at this one guy—Chester. This big guy—he was kind of a little slow. You always had to tell him things two or three times. Anyway, Mr. Campbell looks at the back of his head for a long time while Chester is working—and all a sudden Mr. Campbell

50

says—excuse my language, you're a lawman, so I've got to tell you the exact words—he says 'You son of a bitch'—and he smacks Chester right in the head with the shovel. Well everyone is standing there shocked. And nobody stops him, you know. The other guys all just stand around because it's Mr. Campbell."

"Sure."

"And even when his wife asked him about it, he got mad all over again. You couldn't tell those people anything. You just didn't turn your back on Mr. Campbell."

"So when the maid saw him with a knife and standing over his wife, it was reasonable to think he was stabbing her."

"It was reasonable to think he was stabbing her because he was stabbing her. He was swinging the knife."

"Ah."

"Right. No one tells that story, huh? The maid who stopped him—that was Paola Cardoza—she told my mother the whole thing, which is probably why Mama got deported. They got rid of anybody who could really say anything."

"How was Paola able to kill a grown man like that?"

"She grew up slaughtering sheep, I think. Listen, you should do yourself a favor and get rid of that friend of yours. The Campbells always end up getting everybody running around for them."

"You should've told me that six months ago."

The trial of Angelo Galvan, Jaime Latigua and Michael Smith dragged on for months—or rather the delays of the trial dragged on. The suspects remained in county lock-up and the court stood adjourned as the prosecution filed one delay after another—presumably hoping some actual evidence would appear in the clouds. Finally, more than half a year after the charges were filed, the judge quietly dropped them.

Then, just as quietly, the deportation process began.

I myself only found out about it by accident, when the judge's clerk called, confusing my number with Dan's. I tried getting into the hearing, towing Anne along. But it was a closed session—purely administrative. Anne and I sat outside the courtroom on a wooden bench that, as I recall, used to be the oldest tree in a 20-mile radius. Everything smelled like Pine Sol.

In a little less than an hour, the session adjourned, and deportation was cleared for all three men. Not that there wasn't a bulletproof case for it. I suspect none of them had proper documentation. But that's true of a lot of people. Generally no one cares, until one day someone suddenly does.

The Campbells have a distinct family trait—a line across the bridge of the nose that looks almost like a small crack. Anne has it, and I thought it was just wishful thinking when I saw it on a white-and-red-haired man walking out of the hearing. But I guess I should have known when I saw how he spoke to people, as if they were presumed to listen.

Anne sat up straighter. Of course, she often thought a lot of people were a lot of other people. But this time she had it right. The man saw Anne and walked right to us, taking one of her hands in both of his.

"It's taken care of," he said. "Those men can't hurt you."

She thanked him politely, as if he were handing her an Easter egg. I doubt she cared what he was talking about.

"You're the sheriff who found her?" he said to me. Sherman Campbell. Had to be.

"You're a hard guy to reach," I said.

"Well, we appreciate all you've done for Anne. I wish we could've done more for her."

"You did buy her an entire house," I said. "That's a lot."

"We couldn't put these men in jail. At least they'll be gone from our lives."

"What do you suppose they did?" I said. "I mean, whatever they did."

The transformation was more or less instant. His cheeks turned patchy, his voice cracked, and I instinctively touched my belt where my gun usually hung.

"Mr. Mulliner," he said, ignoring my title as sheriff, but I'm a big enough man to let that go, "We're fierce protectors of our homes. These men drove one of us into the streets."

"Anne," I said, "What did these three men do?"

She smiled up at Sherman as if he were the sun. "They drove us into the streets," she said. She and Sherman nodded to each other. "I couldn't go home."

I looked at her with my mouth open, like a TV comedian. So that was the cue she was waiting for. She just needed one of the popular kids from the mansion to come along, and she'd know what to say. If Sherman blamed her problems on a dead weed, Anne would have sworn to it in court.

With the next week or so, Anne was taken off my hands and given another house, this time uncontaminated by suspicious handymen—and the United States deported three foreign nationals so the Campbells wouldn't have to admit that insanity ran in the family.

13.

For what it's worth—and it's worth something to me, which shows how petty I am—the Broken Hat Sheriff's Department beat the original Broken Hat Police Department, outlasting it by about two days.

A stray job application I'd filled out for the federal Bureau of Land Management finally landed on the right desk, and they called me with a position down near Palm Springs, cruising the desert, tracking down people who dumped garbage and generally keeping a big, dry patch of land from being ruined by idiots. That suited the heck out of me. I'd have to give up my farm out here, but Anne had been right about it. I didn't really have time to take care of it properly and the place was an unkempt embarrassment.

I wasn't going to tell Dan, wasn't going to give him the satisfaction. But then I drove by the Barsden house and saw the moving van. I pulled up, got out, and ended up telling him everything, just so he didn't think I was there to gloat.

He said, "The company has a place for me at some farming community up north."

"Ah. Where they're merging the farms."

"It's going to be a little small for us," he said.

"They gave you an impossible job," I said. "You couldn't

convict some guys who didn't do anything. Why don't you go off and be a real cop some place?"

"Minor heart irregularity," he said.

"It shouldn't matter to anything," Rita piped in. Her pregnancy was beginning to show. "It doesn't slow him down. But they find out about these things."

Dan wanted to change the subject. "I guess you'll have an easier time moving," he said. "No kids. You don't have to think about schools." I could see Rita shake her head slightly to that.

"Pleasures of the poor," I said. "I'm going to get rid of my furniture and just take what fits in the truck. I guess I live like I'm always kind of half waiting to get up and leave."

We talked about a few innocuous things—the houses up north, baseball teams, TV reception. Then we shook hands and I drove off, with Rita watching, as confused by me as the day we met.

When I look back on it now, Dan and Rita are the only people from that town that I still think about a little—the only people I really knew by the end. I mean Anne turned out to be a disappointment. Leonard Fahey started off as an obvious fraud and somehow became even more fraudulent. But Dan and Rita were just trying to please some people who shouldn't have mattered—and that was something I understood. As for the rest of Broken Hat, though—once that place turned from a ranch into a town, my life was like a book I was forced to read, or a rumor I heard about someone else.

I'll tell you a funny story. A few days later when I finally moved away, I actually got lost on my way out of town. Once again, I had unconsciously been using some boarded-up building as a landmark, and suddenly the place wasn't there. In this case, it was the old Campbell mansion. The scene of the Great Stabbing, Broken Hat's only legend, had been leveled. A sign announced they were putting up a new supermarket and a broasted chicken place. I thought that was kind of too bad, but I also thought that having a broasted chicken place nearby would be very convenient.